VITALIS
Prague

BIBLIOTHECA BOHEMICA

The Metamorphosis

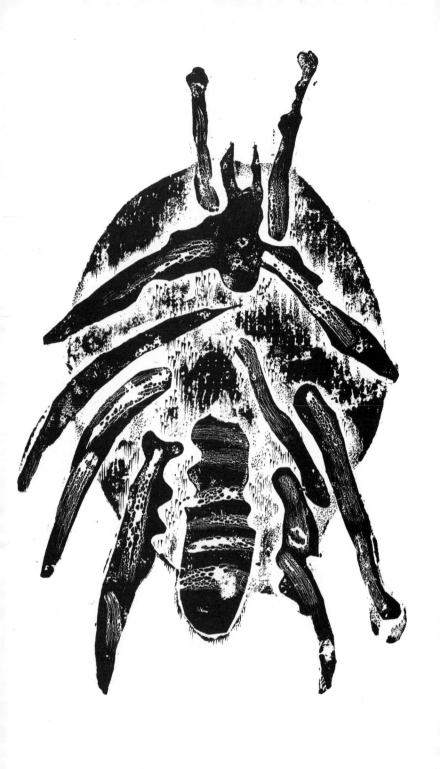

Franz Kafka

THE METAMORPHOSIS

Including
"The Retransformation of Gregor Samsa"
by
Karl Brand

VITALIS
Prague

© Vitalis, 2002
U Železné lávky 568/10
CZ-118 00 Praha
www.vitalis-verlag.com

Translation Karen Reppin
Editor Marc Reppin
Illustrations Karel Hruška
Print Finidr, Český Těšín

ISBN 80-85938-39-1

I

When Gregor Samsa awoke one morning from troubled dreams he found himself transformed in his bed into a monstrous insect. He lay on his back, which was as hard as an armour plate, and saw, as he raised his head a little, his vaulted brown belly divided by stiff, arch-shaped ribs, and the bed covers which could hardly cling to its height and were about to slide off completely. His many legs, pitifully thin compared with the rest of his bulk, waved about helplessly before his eyes.

"What has happened to me?" he thought. It was no dream. His room, an ordinary though somewhat small room for one person, lay peacefully between the four familiar walls. Above the table, on which an unpacked assortment of cloth samples was spread about – Samsa was a commercial traveller – hung the picture which he had recently cut out of a glossy magazine and placed in a pretty gilt frame. It depicted a lady dressed up in a fur hat and stole, sitting upright and raising up toward the viewer a heavy fur muff into which her entire forearm had disappeared.

Gregor's gaze then directed itself to the window, and the overcast weather – he could hear raindrops beating on the metal window-ledge – made him quite melancholy. "What if I just slept a little longer and forgot all this nonsense," he thought, but this was utterly impracticable for he was used to sleeping on his right side and couldn't in his present state get into that position. No matter how vigorously he threw himself onto his right side he always rocked onto his back again. He must have tried it a hundred times, closing his eyes so as not to have to see his squirming legs, and only gave up when he began to feel a slight, dull pain in his side, which he had never felt before.

"Oh God," he thought. "What an exhausting job I've chosen! Day in, day out on the road. The business irritations are much worse than they are in the home office, and in addition, I've got the problems of travel inflicted upon me, with its anxieties about train connections, the irregular, terrible meals, and the constantly changing faces which never develop into lasting, sincere relationships. To hell with it all!" He felt a slight itching on top of his belly, edged himself slowly on his back toward the bedpost so as to be able to lift his head better, found the itchy spot, which was covered with a myriad of small white spots which he didn't know how to interpret; he wanted to touch the spot with one leg but withdrew it immediately for the contact sent a cold shiver through him.

He slid back into his previous position. "This business of rising early," he thought, "makes an idiot out of anyone. People need their sleep. Other travellers live like the women of a harem. For instance, when I go back to the guesthouse during the morning to write up the orders I've secured, these gentle-men are just sitting down to the breakfast table. I should try that with my boss; I'd be fired on the spot. Anyway, who knows if that wouldn't be just the right thing for me. If I weren't holding back because of my parents, I'd have quit long ago; I'd have marched up to the boss and told him straight from the heart what I thought of him. He'd have fallen from his desk! It's curious too how he sits on his desk and talks down from on high to his em-ployees, especially since they have to stand very close to him because of his being hard of hearing. Well, I haven't given up all hope yet; once I have the money together to pay off my parents' debt to him – it should take another five or six years – I'll do it without fail. I'll make a clean break. In the meantime, though, I'd better get up, as my train leaves at five o'clock."

And he looked over at the alarm clock which was ticking on the chest of drawers. "God in heaven!" he thought. It was six thirty, and the hands were moving quietly on, in fact, it was after half past; it was nearly a quarter to seven. Could it be the alarm hadn't gone off? One could see from the bed that it was correctly set for four o'clock; it had surely gone off, too. Yes, but was it possible to sleep quietly through a din that made the furniture shake? Well, he certainly hadn't slept peacefully, but prob-ably the more soundly for it. But what should he do now? The next train left at seven o'clock; in order to catch that one he'd have to be in a frantic haste, and the samples were not yet packed, and he himself wasn't feeling especially fresh and active. And even if he did catch the train, the boss's fury could not be avoided, for the messenger would have been waiting for the five o'clock train and would long since have reported his failure to arrive. He was a tool of the boss, spineless and without any sense. What if he reported sick? That would be terribly embarrassing and look suspicious, for Gregor had never once in his five years of employment been ill. The boss would be sure to arrive with the health insurance doctor, reproach his parents for their lazy son, and cut short all excuses by referring to the insurance doctor, for whom after all only perfectly healthy but work-shy people existed. And besides, would he have been so very wrong in this case? Gregor felt quite fine in fact, with the exception of his drowsiness, superfluous after such a long sleep, and he even had an especially hearty appetite.

As he was thinking all this over at top speed, without being able to force himself out of bed – the alarm clock had just struck a quarter to seven – there was a cautious knock on the door at the head of his bed. "Gregor," called a voice – it was his mother – "it's a quarter to seven. Didn't you have a train to catch?" That soft voice! Gregor got a shock when he heard his voice answering, unmistakably his own voice from before, it was true, but in which an irrepressible, painful squeaking was mixed in with it as if from below, which retained the clarity of his words only for the first moment, before distorting them so much that one could not be sure if one had heard correctly. Gregor had wanted to answer in detail and explain everything, but given the circumstances confined himself to saying, "Yes, yes, thank you mother – I'm just getting up." Because of the wooden door, the change in Gregor's voice was apparently not noticeable from outside, for his mother contented herself with this explanation and shuffled away. But as a result of this brief exchange the other family members had become aware that Gregor was still at home, contrary to all expectations, and already his father was knocking on one of the side-doors, gently but with his fist. "Gregor, Gregor," he called, "what's the matter?" And after a little while he admonished him once more in a deeper voice, "Gregor, Gregor!" Meanwhile, at the other side-door his sister pleaded softly, "Gregor? Aren't you well? Do you need anything?" Gregor answered in both directions, "I'm just about ready," taking care to remove anything conspicuous from his voice by enunciating carefully and inserting long pauses between each word. His father returned to his breakfast, but his sister whispered, "Gregor, open up, I beg you." But Gregor had no intention of opening up at all, rather he congratulated himself for the precautions he had acquired from his travels of locking all doors at night, even at home.

The first thing he wanted was to get up quietly and unbothered, get dressed, and above all have breakfast, and only then consider the rest, for he was well aware that he would not arrive at any sensible conclusions by pondering in bed. He remembered often having experienced a slight pain in bed, perhaps caused by lying in an awkward position, which turned out, once he got up, to be a mere illusion, and he was eager to see how today's fantasy would gradually dissolve. He didn't doubt for a moment that the change in his voice was nothing more than the first sign of a considerable cold, an occupational hazard of the commercial traveller.

Throwing off the bed covers was very easy; he had only to inflate himself a little, and they fell off on their own. But after that it became difficult, especially since he was so unusually wide. He would have needed arms and hands to raise himself; instead he had only these numerous little legs which were in constant, varied motion, and over which he had no control. If he wanted to bend one of them, then it was the first to straighten itself; and if he finally succeeded in getting this leg to perform what he wanted, all the others worked in the meantime as if set free in the most intensely painful agitation. "There's just no point lying around idly," Gregor said to himself.

First he tried to get out of bed with the lower part of his body, but this lower part, which by the way he had not yet seen and which he could not visualize very clearly, proved itself too difficult to manoeuvre; it was going so slowly; and when he finally, having become almost frantic, thrust himself forward recklessly with all the strength he could muster, he had chosen the wrong direction and struck sharply against the lower bedpost. The searing pain he felt informed him that precisely the lower part of his body was perhaps the most sensitive at the moment.

So he tried getting the upper part of his body out and turned his head cautiously toward the edge of the bed. This proved easy enough, and in spite of its width and weight, the mass of his body at last slowly followed the turn of his head. But when he finally held his head over the edge of the bed in the air he became too afraid to continue advancing in this manner for, if he let himself fall in this position, it would take nothing short of a miracle if his head were not to be injured. And at no cost could he lose consciousness now; he would rather stay in bed.

But when after similar efforts he lay there as before, panting, and once more saw his little legs struggling with each other more fiercely than ever, if that were possible, and saw no way of bringing peace and order to this arbitrary confusion, he told himself again that it was impossible for him to stay in bed and that the most sensible thing was to sacrifice everything for even the smallest hope of freeing himself of his bed. At the same time, however, he didn't forget to keep reminding himself that the coolest deliberation was far better than any desperate decisions. At such moments he fixed his eyes as sharply as possible on the window, but unfortunately there was little encouragement or cheer to be had from the sight of the morning fog which shrouded even the other side of the narrow street. "Seven o'clock already," he told himself at the renewed sounding of the alarm clock, "seven o'clock already and still such a fog." And for a little while longer he lay quietly, breathing faintly, as though perhaps expecting from the complete silence a return to real and normal conditions.

But then he said to himself: "Before it strikes a quarter past seven, I positively have to be out of bed without fail. Besides, by then someone from the firm will have come to ask about me since the office opens before seven." And he set about rocking the full length of his body evenly out of bed. If he let himself fall out of bed in this manner, his head, which he intended to lift abruptly on falling, would presumably escape injury. His back appeared to be hard; it was unlikely that a fall onto the carpet would cause any harm. His greatest cause for concern was the loud crash which would certainly result and probably cause anxiety if not alarm behind all the doors. Nonetheless, this would have to be risked.

When Gregor was already jutting halfway out of

bed – the new method was more a game than an effort; he had only to keep rocking back and forth – it occurred to him how simple everything would be if someone came to his assistance. Two strong people – he thought of his father and the servant girl – would have been more than sufficient. They would only have to slide their arms under his vaulted back, scoop him out of bed like that, bend down with their burden, and be careful and patient while he executed a somersault onto the floor, where his little legs would then hopefully derive a purpose. Well, apart from the fact that the doors were locked, should he really call for help? In spite of his predicament he could not suppress a smile at this thought.

He had already reached the point where he could hardly keep his balance anymore with all this vigorous rocking and would very soon have to commit himself - for in five minutes it would be a quarter past seven - when the doorbell rang. "That's someone from the office," he said to himself and almost froze, while his little legs only danced all the faster. For a moment everything remained quiet. "They're not going to open the door," Gregor said to himself, gripped by some insane hope. But then, of course, the servant girl went to the door as usual, with her firm step, and opened it. Gregor had only to hear the visitor's first word of greeting to know at once who it was, the chief clerk himself. Why ever was Gregor condemned to work at a firm where the merest slip immediately attracted the gravest suspicion? Were all the employees scoundrels without exception; was there not one loyal, dedicated person among them who, if he didn't devote a few hours of the morning to the firm, would go crazy with remorse and be actually incapable of getting out of bed? Would it really not have been enough to send an apprentice to inquire, if this inquiring were necessary at all? Did the chief clerk himself have to come, and did the whole innocent family have to be shown by this that the investigation of this suspicious affair could only be entrusted to his judgement alone? And more as a result of the agitation produced by these thoughts than as the result of any real decision, Gregor swung himself out of bed with all his might. There was a loud thud, but it was not really a crash. The fall was to some extent broken by the carpet, and his back was also more elastic than he had thought, hence the not very noticeable muffled sound. Only he hadn't held his head carefully enough and had banged it; he turned it and rubbed it on the carpet in vexation and pain.

"Something fell in there," said the chief clerk in the room on the left. Gregor tried to imagine whether something like what had happened to him today couldn't one day happen to the chief clerk; one certainly had to admit the possibility of this. But as if in brusque reply to this question the chief clerk took a few determined steps in the next room making his patent leather boots creak. From the room on the right his sister whispered to inform Gregor. "Gregor, the chief clerk is here." "I know," said Gregor to himself, but he did not dare raise his voice enough for his sister to hear.

"Gregor," said his father now from the room on the left, "the chief clerk has arrived and is inquiring why you didn't catch the early train. We don't know what to tell him. Besides, he wants to speak to you in person, so please open the door. He will no doubt be good enough to excuse the mess in your room." "Good morning, Mr. Samsa," the chief clerk meanwhile called out in a friendly voice. "He is not well," said his mother to the chief clerk, while his father was still speaking at the door, "he's not well, believe me, sir. How else could Gregor have missed his train! The boy has nothing on his mind but work. It almost exasperates me the way he never goes out in the evening; he's been here in town the last eight days but has been at home every single evening. He just sits with us at the table quietly reading the paper or studying the railway timetables. It's even a distraction for him when he busies himself with his fretwork. For example, in the course of two or three evenings, he whittled a small picture-frame; you will marvel at how pretty it is. It's hanging in his room; you will see it the moment Gregor opens the door. You know, I'm glad you've come, sir. We would never have managed to get Gregor to open the door by ourselves;

he's so stubborn. And I'm sure he's not well, even though he said he was fine this morning." "I'll be right there," said Gregor slowly and deliberately, not moving so as not to miss a word of the conversation. "I can't think of any other explanation either, madam," said the chief clerk. "I hope it's nothing serious. Though I must say on the other hand that we business people, fortunately or unfortunately, as you wish, very often simply have to overcome any slight indisposition out of business considerations." "So, can the chief clerk come in now?" asked his father impatiently, knocking on the door again. "No," said Gregor. An embarrassing silence fell in the room on the left; in the room on the right, his sister began to sob.

Why didn't his sister join the others? She had probably just got out of bed and hadn't even started to dress yet. And why was she crying anyway. Because he didn't get up and let the chief clerk in, because he was in danger of losing his job and because the boss would start hounding his parents again about those old debts? Surely, those were unnecessary worries at present. Gregor was still here and hadn't the slightest intention of deserting his family. True, at the moment he was lying there on the carpet, and nobody familiar with his condition could seriously have expected him to let the chief clerk in. But this slight discourtesy, for which an appropriate explanation could easily be found later on, could hardly mean Gregor's dismissal. And it seemed to Gregor that it would be far more sensible to leave him in peace for now, than to bother him with crying and entreaties. But it was precisely the uncertainty which was distressing the others and which excused their behavior.

"Mr. Samsa," the chief clerk now called with a raised voice, "what's the matter? You barricade yourself in your room, give only 'yes' or 'no' answers, cause your parents a great deal of unnecessary worry, and neglect – this just mentioned in passing – your duties to the firm in an outrageous manner. I am speaking here in the name of your parents and your employer and ask you in all seriousness for an immediate and clear explanation. I'm amazed, amazed. I had always believed you to be a quiet, sensible person, and now you suddenly seem bent on making a strange spectacle of yourself. The boss did suggest to me early this morning a possible explanation for your failure to show up – it had to do with the authority to collect payments which we recently entrusted to you – but I practically gave my word of honour that this explanation could not be right. But now that I see your incredible obstinacy, I'm quickly losing all desire to stick up for you in any way whatsoever, and your job is by no means assured. I originally intended to tell you this in private, but since you make me waste my time here so uselessly I don't see why your parents shouldn't hear it as well. Your performance of late has been very unsatisfactory; this is admittedly not the best season for doing exceptional business, this we grant you; but a season for doing no business at all, such a thing does not exist, Mr. Samsa, cannot be allowed to exist." "But sir," cried Gregor, beside himself and in his agitation forgetting everything else, "I'm just opening up, this very minute. A slight indisposition, a dizzy spell, has kept me from getting up. I'm still lying in bed, but now I'm feeling quite fine again. I'm just getting out of bed. Just be patient for a moment longer! I'm not quite so well yet as I thought, but I'm all right, really. How something like this can just take a person by surprise. Only last night I felt fine, my parents can tell you, or rather, last night I had a slight premonition. I must have shown some sign of it. Why didn't I report it to the firm! But one always thinks that one can weather an illness without staying at home. Sir! Spare my parents! There is no basis for all the accusations you are making against me now; no one has ever mentioned a word about them to me before. Perhaps you have not yet seen the last orders I sent in. Anyway, I'll still catch the eight o'clock train; these few hours of rest have done me good. Don't let me detain you, sir; I'll be at the office in no time, and please be so kind as to tell this to those concerned and to give my respects to the boss!"

And while Gregor hastily blurted all this out and hardly knew what he was saying, he had managed quite easily as a result of the practice he had already acquired in bed to reach the wardrobe, and he now tried to raise himself up against it. He meant to actually open the door, to actually show himself and speak to the chief clerk; he was eager to find out what the others, who were all so anxious to see him, would say at the sight of him. If they were shocked, then he would bear no further responsibility and could rest quietly. But if they took it all calmly, then he had no reason to get excited either and could, if he hurried, actually be at the train station by eight o'clock. At first he slid off the polished surface of the wardrobe a few times, but at last, giving himself a final heave, he stood upright; he no longer paid any attention to the pain in his abdomen, however it burned. Now he let himself fall against the back of a nearby chair, clinging onto the edge of it with his little legs. With that he gained control of himself and fell silent; for now he could listen to what the chief clerk was saying.

"Did you understand a single word of that?" the chief clerk was asking his parents. "He's not trying to make a fool of us, is he?" "Oh, God," cried his mother, already in tears, "perhaps he's seriously ill and we're tormenting him. Grete! Grete!" she then cried. "Mother?" called his sister from the other side. They were communicating through Gregor's room. "You must get the doctor immediately. Gregor is ill. Hurry, run for the doctor. Did you hear how Gregor was speaking just now?" "That was the voice of an animal," said the chief clerk, noticeably softer in comparision to the shrieking of his mother. "Anna! Anna!" his father yelled through the front hall to the kitchen, clapping his hands, "fetch a locksmith at once!" And already the two girls were running, skirts swishing, through the hall – how could his sister have got dressed so quickly? – and tearing open the front door. There was no sound of the door slamming shut at all; they must have left it open, as is the custom in houses where some great misfortune has occurred.

But Gregor had become much calmer. It was apparent that his words were no longer intelligible even though they seemed clear enough to him, clearer than before, perhaps because his ear had grown accustomed to them. In any case, the others now believed that there was something wrong with him, and were prepared to help. The confidence and assurance with which the first instructions had been issued comforted him. He felt himself drawn once more into the human circle and hoped for great and amazing results from both the doctor and the locksmith, without actually distinguishing precisely between them. In order to make his voice as clear as possible for the crucial discussions that were now imminent, he coughed a little, taking care to do so as quietly as he could since this noise too might already sound different from the human cough, something he no longer felt competent to judge. It had in the meantime become completely still in the next room. Perhaps his parents were sitting at the table with the chief clerk, whispering; perhaps they were all leaning against the door and listening.

Gregor pushed himself slowly to the door holding onto the chair, let go of it and threw himself at the door, against which he supported himself – the pads at the ends of his legs were a little sticky – and rested there for a moment from the strain. Then he set about turning the key in the lock with his mouth. Unfortunately, it seemed that he had no real teeth – what should he grip the key with? – but his jaws, on the other hand, were certainly very strong; with their help he actually managed to get the key moving and paid no attention to the fact that he was undoubtedly doing himself some damage, for a brown liquid came out of his mouth, flowed over the key and dripped onto the floor. "Listen," said the chief clerk in the next room, "he's turning the key." That was a great encouragement to Gregor, but they should have all been cheering him on, even his father and mother: "Go, Gregor," they should have shouted, "keep at it, keep turning that key!" And picturing them all following his efforts with suspense, he clenched his jaw desperately on the key with all the strength he could muster. As the turning of the key progressed, he danced around the lock; by now he was holding himself only by his mouth, and either hung himself on the key or pressed it down again with the entire weight of his body, as the situation demanded. The clear sound of the lock snapping back positively woke Gregor up. With a sigh of relief, he said to himself: "So, I didn't need the locksmith," and laid his head on the handle to open the door wide.

Since he had to use this method of opening the door, it was actually open quite wide before he himself could be seen. He had first to edge himself slowly around the one section of the door and do so very carefully indeed if he didn't exactly want to fall flat on his back just at the entrance to the room. He was still engaged with this difficult manoeuvre, and had no time to attend to anything else, when he heard the chief clerk utter a loud "Oh!" – it sounded like a gust of wind – and now he could see him too, standing nearest to the door, as he clasped his hand over his open mouth and slowly retreated as though he were being driven away by an invisible, steady force. His mother – in spite of the presence of the chief clerk, was standing there with her hair still let down after the night and sticking out in all directions – looked first with clasped hands at his father, then took two steps toward Gregor and sank down into the midst of her skirts which were spread out around her, her face completely hidden on her breast. His father clenched a fist with a hostile expression as if he wanted to beat Gregor back into his room, then looked uncertainly around the living room, covered his eyes with his hands and wept such that his mighty chest shook.

Gregor didn't go into the room at all now, but

leaned from inside against the firmly bolted section of the door, so that only half of his body was visible, with his head tilted above it to one side, peering out at the others. It had in the meantime become much lighter. A section of the endlessly long, dark-grey building on the opposite side of the street – it was a hospital – was clearly visible now, with its regular rows of windows starkly punctuating the façade; the rain was still falling, but only in huge separately visible drops that seemed to be literally flung individually to the earth. The breakfast dishes were laid out lavishly on the table, for breakfast was for Gregor's father the most important meal of the day, which he lingered over for hours while reading through a variety of newspapers. Right on the wall opposite hung a photograph of Gregor from his time in the military, which portrayed him as a lieutenant with his hand on his sword and a carefree smile, commanding respect for his bearing and his uniform. The door to the hall was open and one could see, as the front door was also open, out onto the landing and the top of the stairs going down.

"Well," said Gregor, well aware of the fact that he was the only one who had retained any composure, "I'll get dressed right away, pack up the samples and be off. Do you want, do you really want to let me go? Now you see, sir, I'm not stubborn and I enjoy working; travelling is a strain, but I couldn't live without it. Where are you going, sir?

To the office? Yes? Will you give an honest account of all this? One can be temporarily incapacitated, but that is precisely the right time to remember past achievements and to bear in mind that later, after the obstacle has been removed, one will surely work with all the more diligence and concentration. I am so very obligated to the boss, as you know quite well. On the other hand, I also have to provide for my parents and sister. I'm in a fix, but I'll work myself out of it again. But please don't make things any more difficult for me than they already are. Take my side at the office! Travellers aren't popular, I know. People think they earn a fortune and just have a great old time. No one has any particular reason for examining this prejudice more closely. But you, sir, have a better grasp of things than the rest of the staff; yes, in fact quite confidentially stated, a better grasp than the boss himself, who in his capacity as employer can easily allow his judgements to be swayed against an employee. You also know very well that the traveller, who is out of the office almost the whole year round, can so easily fall victim to gossip, bad luck, and unfounded complaints – against which he is quite unable to defend himself, since he usually never learns about them, and only then when he returns home, exhausted from one of his journeys, is he made to feel the the terrible consequences on his own person, but can no longer trace what caused them. Sir, don't leave without a word to me which shows me that you consider me even partially right!"

But the chief clerk had already turned away at Gregor's first words and only stared back at him over his twitching shoulder and gaping mouth. He never stood still for a moment during Gregor's speech, but rather, without letting Gregor out of his sight, retreated toward the door, yet very gradually as though there remained some secret prohibition against leaving the room. He was already in the hall and, judging by the sudden movement with which he took his last step out of the living room, one could have believed that he had just burned the sole of his foot. Once in the hall, however, he stretched his right hand far out towards the staircase, as though there awaited him nothing short of divine deliverance.

Gregor understood that the chief clerk must on no account be allowed to leave in this frame of mind if his position with the firm were not to be severely jeopardized. His parents did not understand this so well; they had formed the convinction over the course of the years that Gregor was set for life in this firm, and besides, were so preoccupied with their immediate troubles that all foresight had left them. But Gregor had this foresight. The chief clerk must be detained, soothed, persuaded and finally won over; the future of Gregor and his family depended on it! If only his sister had been there! She was clever; she had already begun to cry while

Gregor was still lying quietly on his back. And no doubt the chief clerk, this ladies' man, would have been swayed by her; she would have shut the front door and talked him out of his fright in the hall. But his sister was not there, and Gregor had to act on his own. And without thinking that he still didn't know what his powers of movement were, without even considering that his words had possibly – indeed, probably – not even been understood, he let go of the section of the door and pushed himself through the opening; he started to walk toward the chief clerk, who was already ridiculously clutching the railing of the landing with both hands. Immediately after searching for a foothold, Gregor fell down with a small cry onto his numerous little legs. Hardly had this happened when he experienced a sense of physical well-being for the first time this morning; his legs were on solid ground, and they obeyed him perfectly, which he noted with joy. They even strove to carry him off wherever he wanted to go, and he already believed that the end of all his sufferings was imminent. But at that very moment as he lay there on the floor rocking with restrained motion, not at all far from his mother and directly opposite her, she – who had seemed so completely self-absorbed – suddenly jumped to her feet, her arms outstretched, her fingers splayed, and cried "Help, for God's sake, help!" craned her head forward as if to see Gregor better, yet on the contrary backed senselessly away from him. She had

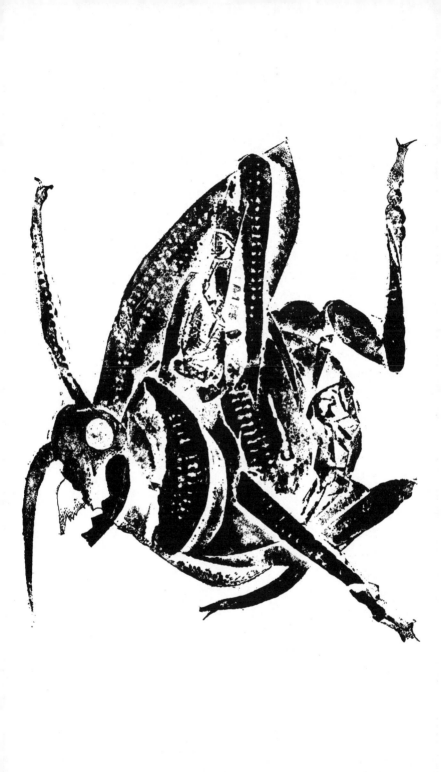

forgotten that the laden table stood behind her, sat down on it hastily and absent-mindedly when she approached it, and seemed altogether unaware that the big coffee pot had toppled over and was pouring coffee in a steady stream onto the carpet.

"Mother, mother," said Gregor softly, and looked up at her. The chief clerk had momentarily slipped his mind completely; on the other hand, he couldn't resist snapping his jaws in the air at the sight of the flowing coffee. At that his mother screamed anew, fled from the table and fell into the arms of his father who came hurrying toward her. But Gregor had no time to spare for his parents just now; the chief clerk was already on the stairs; with his chin on the banister, he was taking one last look back. Gregor charged towards him to be as sure as possible of catching up to him; the chief clerk must have anticipated as much for he leapt down several steps in one bound and disappeared, but he was still yelling, 'Aagh!' and it echoed through the whole staircase. Unfortunately, this flight of the chief clerk seemed to confuse his father completely, who had up until now remained relatively composed, for instead of running after the man himself, or at least not hindering Gregor in his pursuit, he seized in his right hand the chief clerk's walking stick, which he had left behind together with his hat and overcoat, grabbed a large newspaper from the table with his left hand and, stamping his feet, set about driving Gregor back into his room by flourishing the stick and newspaper. No amount of pleading could help Gregor, indeed no pleading was understood; however humbly he turned his head, his father only stamped all the harder. Across the room, his mother had torn open a window in spite of the cold weather and was leaning far out of it with her face buried in her hands. A strong draft swept between the alley and the staircase, the curtains blew in, the newspapers on the table rustled, and single sheets fluttered across the floor. Relentlessly his father drove him back, making hissing noises like a savage. Now Gregor was still unpractised in walking backwards, and it really went rather slowly. If Gregor had only been permitted to turn around, he would have been in his room at once, but he was afraid of infuriating his father by this time-consuming rotation, while at any moment the stick in his father's hand threatened a deadly blow to the back or head. But in the end Gregor had no other choice, for he had found to his horror that he could not even keep direction in reverse; and thus he began, while constantly throwing anxious side glances at his father, to turn himself around as quickly as he could, which was in reality very slowly. Perhaps his father realized his good intentions, for he did not interfere with him in this, but rather directed the manoeuvre now and then from afar with the tip of his stick. If only his father wouldn't make that unbearable hissing noise! It made Gregor lose his head completely. He had almost completely turned around, when, distracted by this hissing, he even made a mistake and turned back a little. But when at last he had succeeded in getting his head to face the doorway, it was apparent that his body was too wide to get through without problems. Of course it didn't even remotely occur to his father in his present mood to open the other section of the door so as to create a sufficient passage for Gregor. His fixed idea was simply to get Gregor into his room as quickly as possible. Nor would he ever have permitted the complicated preparations which Gregor needed to make in order to stand upright and perhaps get through the door that way. On the contrary, he now drove Gregor on as if there were no obstacle in his path, making an exceptional noise; it no longer sounded like the voice of just one single father behind him; now this was really no joke anymore, and Gregor forced himself – come what may – into the doorway. One side of his body rose up and he lay tilted at an angle in the doorway; his flank was scraped quite sore and horrid blotches stained the white door, he soon got stuck fast and could not by himself have budged any further; his little legs on one side hung trembling in the air, those on the other side were painfully crushed to the floor when his father gave him a hard shove, which was literally a deliverance, and he flew far into the room, bleeding profusely. The door was slammed shut with the stick; then finally all was quiet.

II

Only at dusk did Gregor awaken from his deep sleep, which was more like a swoon. He would certainly not have woken much later without being disturbed, for he felt well enough rested and slept, but it seemed to him that a fleeting step and a cautious shutting of the door leading to the hall had roused him. The light of the electric streetlamps shone palely here and there on the ceiling and the upper parts of the furniture, but down below where Gregor lay it was dark. Slowly, still groping clumsily with his feelers, which he was only now learning to appreciate, he pushed himself toward the door, to see what had been happening there. His left side felt like one single, long, unpleasantly taut scar and he had actually to limp on his two rows of legs. Moreover, one leg had been seriously injured in the course of the morning's events – it was almost a miracle that only one had become injured – and trailed lifelessly behind him.

Only when he got to the door did he discover what had actually enticed him there, it was the smell of something to eat. For there stood a bowl filled with fresh milk in which small slices of whitebread were floating. He could almost have laughed with delight, for he was even hungrier than he had been during the morning, and he immediately dipped his head into the milk to almost over his eyes. But he soon withdrew it again in disappointment; it was not only because he had difficulty eating owing to his tender left side – and he could only eat if his whole panting body co-operated – but because he didn't like the milk either, though it had always been his favorite drink, which was surely why his sister had set it there for him. Indeed it was almost with disgust that he turned away from the bowl and crawled back into the middle of the room.

In the living room the gas was lit, as Gregor could see through the crack in the door, but whereas normally at this time of day his father was in the habit of reading the afternoon paper aloud to his mother and sometimes his sister as well, now not a sound was to be heard. Well, perhaps this practice of reading aloud, which his sister was always telling and writing him about, had recently come to an end. But it was so quiet all around, although the flat certainly was not empty. "What a quiet life the family has been leading," Gregor said to himself, and as he stared ahead into the darkness, he felt very proud that he had been able to provide such a life for his parents and sister in such a lovely flat. But what if all the peace, all the comfort, all the contentment came to a terrible end? Rather than lose himself in such thoughts, Gregor set himself in motion and crawled about the room.

Once during the long evening, the side-doors on either side of the room were opened a crack and quickly closed again; someone had evidently felt the need to enter, but then also had too many second thoughts. Gregor now stationed himself right at the living room door, determined somehow to get the hesitant visitor to come in or at least to discover who it might be, but now the door was not opened again, and Gregor waited in vain. In the morning when the doors had been locked, everyone wanted to come in; now that he had opened one door, and the others had clearly been opened during the day, no one came any more, and the keys were now stuck on the outside too.

It was late at night when the light in the living room was put out, and it was now easy to ascertain that his parents and sister had stayed up until then, for he could clearly hear all three stealing away on tiptoe. It was now certain that no one would come into Gregor's room until morning; consequently he had plenty of time to consider undisturbed how best to reorganize his life. But the high, spacious room in which he was forced to lie flat on the floor frightened him without his being able to say why, for it was, after all, the room he had occupied for the past five years – and with a half-unconscious turn and not without a slight feeling of shame, he scuttled under the sofa where he immediately felt comfortable, even though his back was squeezed a little bit and he could no longer lift his head; his only regret being that his body was too wide for the whole of it to be accommodated under the sofa.

There he stayed the whole of the night, which

he partly spent in a doze from which hunger pangs kept waking him with a start, and partly in worries and vague hopes, all of which, however, led to the conclusion that for the time being he would have to stay calm and, by exercising the utmost consideration, help the family bear the inconvenience he was bound to cause them in his present condition.

Early the next morning – it was still almost night – Gregor had the opportunity to test the strength of his new resolutions, for his sister, almost fully dressed, opened the door of the hall and peered in intently. She did not see him right away, but when she caught sight of him under the sofa – God, he had to be somewhere, he couldn't have just flown away – she was so startled that without being able to control herself she slammed the door shut again. But as though regretting her behavior she opened the door again immediately and came in on tiptoe, as if she was visiting someone gravely ill, or even a stranger. Gregor had pushed his head forward right to the edge of the sofa and was watching her. Would she notice that he had left the milk untouched, and by no means for lack of hunger, and would she bring in some other kind of food which suited him better? If she didn't do it of her own accord, he would rather starve than bring it to her attention, although he felt an enormous urge to shoot out from under the sofa, throw himself at his sister's feet, and beg her for something good to eat.

But his sister noticed immediately, to her surprise, that the bowl was still full, only a little milk had been spilled around. She picked it up immediately, though not with her bare hands of course, but with a rag, and carried it out. Gregor was extremely curious to know what she would bring as a replacement and speculated about the various possibilities. But he could never have guessed what his sister in the goodness of her heart actually did. To find out what he liked, she brought him a wide assortment all spread out on an old newspaper. There were old, half-rotten vegetables; bones from last night's supper, covered with a solidified white sauce; a few raisins and almonds; a piece of cheese that Gregor had declared inedible days ago; a slice of dry bread; a slice of bread and butter; and one with butter and salt. In addition to all this, she set down the bowl now apparently reserved for Gregor, into which she had poured some water. And out of a sense of delicacy, knowing that Gregor would not eat in front of her, she quickly withdrew and even turned the key in the lock so that Gregor should know that he could make himself as comfortable as he wished. Gregor's legs began whirring now that he was going to eat. His wounds must have healed completely by now, for he no longer felt any handicap; this amazed him and he thought of how over a month ago he had cut his finger slightly with a knife and how this wound had still been hurting only the day before yesterday. "Have I become less sensitive now?" he thought, already sucking greedily at the cheese, to which, more than all the other foods, he had been drawn instantly and forcibly. One after the other and with tears of satisfaction welling in his eyes, he quickly consumed the cheese, the vegetables and sauce; the fresh foods, on the other hand, he did not care for. He couldn't even stand the smell of them, and he actually dragged the things he did want to eat a little farther away. He had long since finished with everything and was just lying lazily in the same spot, when his sister slowly turned the key as a sign that he should retreat. This startled him at once, though he was already almost dozing off, and he scuttled back under the sofa again. But it took considerable self-control for him to stay under the sofa, even for the short time his sister was in the room, for his body had become somewhat bloated from the substantial meal, and he could hardly breathe in this confined space. Between slight attacks of suffocation he watched with bulging eyes as his unsuspecting sister took a broom and swept up not only the remains, but also the foods Gregor had not even touched, as if they were no longer usable either, and then dumped everything hastily into a bucket, which she then covered with a wooden lid and carried out. Hardly had she turned her back when Gregor came out from under the sofa, stretching and inflating himself.

Thus Gregor now received his food daily, once

in the morning while his parents and the servant girl were still asleep, and a second time after the midday meal, for then his parents took another short nap and the servant girl would be sent away by his sister on some errand or other. Certainly they did not want Gregor to starve, but perhaps they could not have been able to bear to know any more about his feeding than from hearsay, or perhaps his sister wanted to spare them what were even minor torments, for indeed they really were suffering enough as it was.

Under what pretext the doctor and locksmith had been got rid of that first morning, Gregor could not discover; for since the others could not understand what he said, it never occured to them, not even his sister, that he could understand them; and so whenever his sister was in his room he had to content himself with her occasional sighs and invocations of the saints. It was only later when she had begun to get used to everything a little – of course there was no question of getting completely used to it – Gregor sometimes caught a remark which was meant to be friendly or could be interpreted as such. "Today he really liked it," she would say when Gregor had put away a good helping, whereas in the opposite case, which gradually happened more and more frequently, she would say almost sadly, "This time everything's been left again."

Although Gregor couldn't get any news directly,

he did overhear a lot of things from the neighbouring rooms, and as soon as he heard voices he would run straight to the door in question and press his whole body against it. Especially in the early days there was no conversation that did not in some way refer to him, even if only implicitly. For two whole days there were family consultations at all meal times about what should now be done; but the same topic was also discussed even between meals, for there were always at least two members of the family at home, probably since no one wanted to stay home alone, and to leave the flat completely was unthinkable. And on the very first day, the servant girl – it was not quite clear just what and how much she knew of what had happened – came to his mother on her knees, and begged her to dismiss her immediately, and when she took her leave a quarter of an hour later, she thanked them for the dismissal in tears as if for the greatest blessing that one had bestowed upon her, and without any prompting swore a solemn oath never to divulge even the slightest word about what had happened to anybody.

So now his sister, working together with his mother had to do the cooking too; of course it was no great effort as they hardly ate anything at all. Gregor was always hearing them vainly urging one another to eat and getting no answer but, "Thank you, I've had enough," or something similar. They didn't seem to drink anything, either. His sister often asked his father if he wouldn't like some beer and kindly offered to get it herself, and when he remained silent, she would say to remove any hesitations on his part that she could also send the caretaker for it, but then his father would finally answer with a definite "No," and no more would be said about it.

In the course of the very first day, his father presented the family's financial situation and prospects to both his mother and his sister. Now and then he got up from the table and brought some receipt or notebook out of the little strongbox, which he had rescued from the collapse of his business five years before. One could hear him open the complicated lock, and then, after taking out what he was looking for, lock it once again. These explanations by his father were to some extent the first encouraging things that Gregor had heard since his captivity. He had supposed that nothing in the least had remained of his father's old business; at least, his father had never told him anything to the contrary, and in any case, Gregor had never asked about it. At the time, Gregor's sole concern had been to do his utmost to get the family to forget as quickly as possible the business disaster which had plunged them all into a state of total despair, and so he had begun to work with particular fervour and had risen almost overnight to become a commercial traveller from being a junior clerk with, of course, quite different prospects, and his successes were immediately translated by way of commission into hard cash that could be set down on the table in front of his astonished and delighted family. Those had been happy times, and they had never recurred, at least not in the same splendour, even though Gregor later earned so much money that he was able to meet the expenses of the whole family and even did so. Both the family as well as Gregor had simply become used to it; the money was gratefully accepted and gladly given, but it never gave rise to any special warmth anymore. Only his sister had remained close to Gregor and it was his secret plan that she, who unlike him loved music and could play the violin so movingly, should be sent next year to the Conservatory, regardless of the great expense which this would entail and which could surely be made up for in some other way. Often during Gregor's short stays in the city, the Conservatory would come up in conversations with his sister, but always merely as a beautiful dream which could never be realized, and his parents didn't approve of even these innocent references; but Gregor was determined about it and intended to solemnly announce his plan on Christmas Eve.

Such were the thoughts, rather useless in his present condition, that went through his head as he stood glued to the door, listening. Sometimes out of general weariness he could no longer listen and he would let his head bump carelessly against the door, but he held it up again immediately, for even the slight sound this made was heard next door and left everyone in silence. "What's he up to now?" his father would say after a while, obviously turning toward the door, and only then would the interrupted discussion gradually be resumed.

Gregor was now thoroughly informed – for his father tended to repeat himself in his explanations, partly because it was a long time since he had concerned himself with these matters and partly because his mother didn't always grasp things the first time around – that in spite of all their misfortunes, a certain sum of money, albeit a small one, had survived intact from the old days and had increased a little in the meantime thanks to the untouched interest. Besides that, the money Gregor had brought home every month – he would only keep a few coins for himself – had never been completely used up and had now accumulated into a small capital sum. Behind his door Gregor nodded eagerly, delighted by this unexpected foresight and thrift. Actually, he could have paid off more of his father's debts to the boss with this surplus money, thus bringing the day on which he could have quit his job all the closer, but now things were undoubtedly better the way his father had arranged them.

However, this money was by no means sufficient to enable the family to live off the interest; it sufficed perhaps to keep the family for one or two years at most. It was just a sum which was not to be touched, but rather set aside for an emergency; money to live on had to be earned. Now his father was still a healthy though elderly man who had not worked for the past five years, and who in any case ought not to expect too much of himself. During those five years, his first years of leisure in his hard-working though unsuccessful life, he had put on a lot of weight and had become rather sluggish as a result. And his elderly mother who suffered from asthma, was she to start earning money now, for whom even a walk through the flat was strenuous enough and who spent every second day on the sofa by the open window gasping for breath? And was his sister to go out and work, who at seventeen was still a child, and whose lifestyle of which it would be a shame to deprive her, which had consisted of wearing pretty clothes, sleeping late, helping in the house, enjoying a few modest entertainments, and above all playing the violin? Whenever the conversation turned to the necessity of earning money, Gregor would always let go of the door and throw himself onto the cool leather sofa beside it, for he felt all hot from shame and grief.

Often he would lie there the long nights through, without sleeping a wink and only scrabbling on the leather for hours on end. Or else he would tackle the strenuous task of pushing an armchair to the window, then crawling up to the window sill and propped up in the armchair lean against the window-panes, clearly in some recollection of that sense of freedom that looking out of the window used to give him. For in fact, from day to day he saw things only a short distance away less and less distinctly; he was not able to make out the hospital across the street, the sight of which he used to curse because he saw so much of it, and if he had not known for sure that he lived in the quiet though thoroughly urban Charlotte Street, he might have believed that he was looking out of his window into a wasteland in which the grey sky and the grey earth blended indistinguishably together. It took his observant sister only twice to notice that the armchair was standing by the window; from then on, whenever she'd tidied up the room, she always pushed the armchair back to the same place by the window, and would even leave the inner casements open.

If only Gregor had been able to speak to his sister and thank her for everything she had to do for him, he could have borne her services more easily. But as it was, they opressed him. She certainly tried to ease the embarrassment of the whole business as much as possible, and as time went on she succeeded more and more. But with time Gregor saw things all the more clearly. Even the way she came in was terrible for him. Hardly had she entered the room than she would rush straight to the window without taking any time to close the door, however careful she usually was to spare anyone the sight of Gregor's room, and tear open the casements with impatient fingers almost as though she were suffocating, and remain there a little while by the window, even in the coldest weather, taking deep breaths. With this noise and dashing around she terrified Gregor twice daily; the whole time he cowered under the sofa, and yet he knew very well that she would certainly have spared him this if she had found it possible to stay in the same room as him with the window closed.

One time – it must have been a month since Gregor's transformation, and there was no longer any particular reason for his sister to be astonished at Gregor's appearance – she came a little earlier than usual and found him propped up and looking out of the window, motionless and at his most terrifying. Gregor would not have been surprised if she had decided not to come in, for in this position he prevented her from opening the window, but not only did she not come in, she actually jumped back in alarm and shut the door; a stranger might well have thought that Gregor had been lying in wait for her and had meant to bite her. Of course, he hid himself under the sofa at once, but he had to wait until noon before she returned, and she seemed much more ill-at-ease than normal. This made him realize that the sight of him was still repulsive to her and was bound to go on being repulsive, and that it probably cost her a lot of effort to resist the desire to run away at the sight of even the small portion of his body which protruded from under the sofa. So as to spare her the sight of even this, he one day carried the sheet to the sofa on his back – it took four hours to do this job – and arranged it in such a way that he was now completely covered and his sister would not be able to see him, even if she stooped down. Had she considered this sheet unnecessary, then she could have removed it, of course, since it could obviously not have been to Gregor's amusement to isolate himself so completely, but she left the sheet as it was, and Gregor even believed himself to have glimpsed a thankful look when he carefully raised the sheet a little once with his head to see how his sister was taking the new arrangement.

During the first two weeks his parents could not bring themselves to go into Gregor's room, and he often heard them express their appreciation for his sister's present work, whereas up until then they had been frequently annoyed with her because she had seemed to them a somewhat useless girl. But now both of them, his father and his mother, often waited outside Gregor's room while his sister tidied it up, and as soon as she came out she had to tell them in great detail how it looked in his room, what Gregor had eaten, how he behaved this time, and whether there was perhaps a small noticeable improvement. His mother, moreover, began relatively soon to want to visit Gregor, but his father and sister dissuaded her at first with rational arguments which Gregor listened to very attentively, and thoroughly approved of. But later she had to be restrained by force and when she then cried out: "Let me go to Gregor, he is my unfortunate son! Don't you see that I have to go to him?" Gregor thought that it might perhaps be a good idea after all if his mother did come in, not every day, of course, but perhaps once a week; she really understood things much better than his sister, who for all her courage was still only a child and had, perhaps, when all was said and done, taken on such a difficult task out of childish flightiness.

Gregor's wish to see his mother was soon fulfilled. During the daytime Gregor did not want to show himself at the window, if only out of consideration for his parents, but he couldn't crawl very far on the few square metres of floor space either; he found he could hardly endure lying still even at night, and eating soon ceased to give him even the slightest pleasure; so, as a distraction, he adopted the habit of crawling all over the walls and ceiling. He especially liked hanging from the ceiling; it was quite different from lying on the floor; one could breathe more freely, a slight swinging sensation passed through one's body and in the almost blissful state of absent-mindedness which Gregor found up there, it could happen to his own surprise that he would let go and fall smack onto the floor. But by now, of course, he had much better control over his body than before, and even such a big drop did him no damage. His sister was quick to notice the new entertainment that Gregor had hit upon for himself – he left behind traces of his sticky stuff here and there from crawling – so she took it into her head to provide Gregor with the greatest possible crawling space by clearing away the pieces of furniture that impeded him, in particular the wardrobe and desk. However, she could not manage this herself; she did not dare ask her father for help, and the servant girl would most certainly not have helped her, for this girl of about sixteen had been bravely holding out since the departure of the previous cook, and had asked as a special favour to be allowed to keep the kitchen door locked at all times and open up only when expressly summoned, so his sister had no other choice than to fetch her mother when her father was out. She came indeed with exclamations of eager delight, but fell silent at the door to Gregor's room. First his sister made sure, of course, that everything in the room was in order; only then did she allow her mother to enter. In great haste, Gregor had pulled the sheet still lower and tugged it into more folds; the whole thing really did look just like a sheet casually thrown over the sofa. This time Gregor also refrained from spying from under the sheet; he did without seeing his mother this time around and was only happy that she had even come at all. "Come on in, you can't see him," said his sister, evidently leading her mother by the hand. Gregor could now hear the two frail women shifting the old wardrobe from its place, which was quite heavy indeed, and his sister taking the greater part of the job upon herself, ignoring the warnings of her mother, who feared she would over-exert herself. It took a very long time. After a quarter of an hour of struggle his mother declared that they had better leave the wardrobe where it was, for in the first place it was just too heavy. They would never be finished before his father came home, and the wardrobe in the middle of the room would only block every path for Gregor, and in the second place it wasn't at all certain that they were doing Gregor a favour by removing the furniture. It seemed to her to be the opposite case: the sight of the bare wall was heartbreaking, and why shouldn't Gregor have this same feeling, too, since he had been used to the furniture for so long and would therefore feel abandoned in the empty room. "And wouldn't it look," his mother concluded softly – in fact she had been almost whispering the whole time as if to avoid letting Gregor, whose exact whereabouts she didn't know, hear even the sound of her voice, for she was convinced that he didn't understand her words – "and wouldn't it look as though, by moving the furniture, we were showing him that we're giving up all hope of his recovery and are callously leaving him to his own devices? I think it would be best to try to keep the room exactly as it was before, so that when Gregor comes back to us he will find everything unchanged and can forget all the more easily what has happened in the meantime."

Upon hearing these words of his mother Gregor realized that the lack of any direct human speech in the course of these two months, coupled with the monotonous life among the family, must have confused his mind, for he could not explain to himself in any other way that he could seriously have wanted his room be cleared out. Did he really want his warm room, so comfortably fitted with family furniture, to be turned into a cave, in which, of course, he would be able to freely crawl about unimpeded in all directions, yet at the cost of rapidly and completely forgetting his human past at the same time? Indeed, he was already on the verge of forgetting, and only the voice of his mother, which he had not heard for so long, shook him up. Nothing should be removed; everything had to stay. He couldn't do without the good effects of the furniture on his condition, and if the furniture hindered him in carrying on this senseless crawling around then that was no drawback, but rather a great advantage.

But his sister was unfortunately of a different opinion. She had grown accustomed, and not without some justification, to adopting with her parents the role of a special expert in matters concerning Gregor, and so her mother's advice was reason enough for his sister to not only insist on the removal of the wardrobe and the desk, which was all she had intended at first, but also on the removal of all of the furniture, with the exception of the indispensible sofa. It was, of course, not only childish obstinacy and the self-confidence she had recently acquired so unexpectedly and at such cost that led her to this demand. She had, in fact, observed that Gregor needed a lot of space to crawl around in, while on the other hand he made no use of the furniture at all as far as one could see. And perhaps the enthusiastic spirit of girls her age, which seeks to indulge itself at every opportunity, also played a part by tempting her to make Gregor's situation even more horrific, so that she might do even more for him than now. For in a room where Gregor alone ruled the bare walls it was unlikely that anyone besides Grete would ever dare to set foot.

Thus she didn't allow herself to be swayed from her resolve by her mother, who also seemed to feel unsure of herself out of the sheer anxiety of being in this room, and soon fell silent and did as best she could to help her daughter with the removal of the wardrobe. Well, Gregor could do without the wardrobe if need be, but the desk had to stay. And no sooner had the women got the wardrobe out of the room, groaning and pushing, than Gregor stuck his head from under the sofa to see how he could intervene as carefully and considerately as possible. But as luck would have it, it was his mother who returned first while Grete was in the next room with her arms around the wardrobe, swinging it back and forth by herself, without of course budging it an inch. His mother, however, was not used to the sight of Gregor, he might have made her ill, and so Gregor quickly retreated in alarm to the far end of the sofa, but could not prevent the sheet from swaying a little in front. That was enough to put his mother on the alert. She stopped short, stood still for a moment, and then went back to Grete.

Although Gregor kept reassuring himself that nothing out of the ordinary was happening, that a few pieces of furniture were only being rearranged, he soon had to admit that this coming and going of the women, their little calls to each other, the scraping of the furniture on the floor, had the effect upon him of some great turmoil fuelled from all sides, and no matter how much he tucked in his head and legs and pressed his body to the floor, he was forced to conclude that he wouldn't be able to stand all of this much longer. They were clearing out his room; depriving him of everything that was dear to him; they had already carried away the wardrobe in which he kept the fretsaw and other tools; they were now loosening the desk which was already firmly sunk into the floor, the desk at which he had done his homework as a student at the commercial academy, as a grammar school student, yes, even as an elementary school pupil – now he really had no more time to examine the good intentions of the two women, whose existence he had indeed almost forgotten for they were by now working in silence out of sheer exhaustion and one could only hear the heavy shuffling of their feet.

And so he burst forth – the women were just leaning against the desk in the next room to catch their breath a moment – changed direction four times, for he really didn't know what to salvage first, then saw the picture of the woman all dressed up in furs hanging conspicuously on the otherwise bare wall, quickly crawled up to it and pressed himself against the glass, which held him fast and soothed his hot belly. This picture at least, which Gregor now completely covered, would definitely not be taken away by anybody. He turned his head to the door of the living room so as to observe the women on their return.

They had not granted themselves much of a rest and were already coming back; Grete had put her arm around her mother and was practically carrying her. "So, what shall we take now?" said Grete, and looked around. At that her eyes met Gregor's from the wall. Probably only because of the presence of her mother did she retain her composure, bent her head down to her mother to keep her from looking around, and said, although hastily and in a trembling voice: "Come, we'd better go back into the living room for a moment." Grete's intentions were clear enough to Gregor: she wanted to bring her mother to safety and then chase him down from the wall. Well, just let her try! He sat on his picture and would not relinquish it. He would rather fly in Grete's face.

But Grete's words had only made her mother all the more anxious; she stepped aside, caught sight of the huge brown blotch on the flowered wallpaper, and before it really dawned on her that what she saw was Gregor, screamed in a shrill, hoarse voice, "Oh God, oh God!" and collapsed over the sofa with outstretched arms as if giving up, and didn't stir. "You! Gregor!" cried his sister with a raised fist, glaring at him. These were the first words she had directly addressed to him since his transformation. She ran into the next room to find some sort of essence with which to revive her mother; Gregor wanted to help too – there was still enough time to rescue his picture – but he was stuck fast to the glass and had to tear himself loose by force; then he too ran into the next room as if he could give his sister some advice, as in earlier days; but then had to stand idly behind her; while she was rummaging among various little bottles she turned around and gave a start of alarm; a bottle fell to the floor and broke, a splinter of glass wounded Gregor in the face and some kind of corrosive medicine splashed around him. Now Grete, without further delay, took as many little bottles as she could hold and ran with them to her mother, slamming the door shut with her foot. Gregor was now cut off from his mother, who was perhaps nearly dying because of him, and he dared not open the door for fear of chasing away his sister, who had to stay with his mother; there was nothing he could do now but wait; and beset by self-reproach and worry, he began to crawl, crawled over everything, walls, furniture and ceiling, until finally, in despair as the whole room began to reel around him, he fell down onto the middle of the big table.

A short while elapsed, and Gregor lay there feebly; all around was quiet; perhaps that was a good sign. Then the doorbell rang. The servant girl was of course locked in her kitchen, so Grete had to go and answer. His father had come back. "What happened?" were his first words; Grete's face must have told him everything. Grete answered in a muffled voice, she was obviously pressing her face against her father's chest: "Mother fainted, but she's better now. Gregor broke loose." "Well, I expected as much," said his father, "I've been telling you all along, but you women just won't listen." It was clear to Gregor that Grete's father had taken the worst interpretation from Grete's all too brief summary and assumed Gregor had been guilty of some violent act. Therefore, Gregor now had to try to placate his father, for he had neither time nor the means to explain things to him. And so he fled to the door of his room and pressed himself against it, so that his father could see as soon as he came in from the hall that Gregor had the best intention of returning to his room immediately and that it was not necessary to drive him back; if only the door were opened, he would disappear at once.

But his father was in no mood to notice such subtleties. "Ah!" he yelled upon entering, in a tone that sounded enraged and exulted at the same time. Gregor drew his head back from the door and raised it towards his father. This was really not how he pictured his father as he stood there now; of course, he had been too absorbed of late by this novel crawling fun to bother as much as before about the proceedings in the rest of the flat, and should really have been prepared for some changes. And yet, and yet, was this still his father? The same man who used to lie wearily, buried in bed, whenever Gregor would set out on a business trip; who greeted him on his return home in the evening, reclining in an easy chair and wearing only a bathrobe; who was actually hardly capable of getting up, but only raised his arms as a sign of gladness, and who, on the rare occasion when the whole family went out for a walk a few Sundays a year and on major holidays, walked between Gregor and his mother, who were slow walkers anyway, always a little slower than they, bundled up in his old coat, carefully working his way forward with his crook-handled stick, and whenever he wanted to say something, nearly always stood still and gathered his escort around him? But now he was standing there erect and in fine form, dressed in a tight fitting blue uniform with gold buttons such as

bankmessengers wear, his strong double chin spread out over the high, stiff collar of his jacket; from under his bushy eyebrows his black eyes sent out alert, piercing glances; his usually dishevelled white hair was combed down flat into a scrupulously exact gleaming parting. He pitched his cap, which bore a gold monogram, probably that of a bank, in an arc across the whole room onto the sofa, and with the tails of his long uniform jacket thrown open, and his hands in his pants pockets, advanced with a grim expression toward Gregor. He probably did not know himself what he had in mind; in any case he lifted his feet unusually high, and Gregor was astounded at the enormous size of the soles of his boots. But he did not linger over this, he had known from the very first day of his new life that his father considered only the severest treatment as appropriate for dealing with him. And so he ran ahead of his father, stopping when his father stopped, and hurrying on again at his father's slightest move. In this way they circled the room several times without anything decisive happening. Indeed, the whole operation did not even have the appearance of a chase because it proceeded so slowly. For this reason Gregor stayed on the floor for the time being, especially since he feared his father might regard a flight onto the walls or ceiling as an act of particular malevolence. At any rate, Gregor had to admit that he would not be able to keep up even this running for long, for while his father took one step he had to execute a whole series of movements. He was beginning to feel winded, as indeed, even in his former life, his lungs had never been completely dependable. While staggering around like this, hardly keeping his eyes open to try to concentrate all his energy on running; in his apathy he never thought of any escape other than by running; and having almost forgotten that the walls were available to him, though they were of course obstructed by elaborately carved furniture full of peaks and spikes – suddenly something flew past him, something lightly tossed, and rolled in front of him. It was an apple, a second one followed immediately. Gregor stopped dead in terror: further running was pointless, for his father was determined to bombard him. He had filled his pockets from the fruit bowl on the side-board and was now throwing one apple after another, so far without taking careful aim. These small apples rolled around on the floor as if electrified, striking against each other. One weakly thrown apple grazed Gregor's back, and slid off harmlessly. But another one flying immediately after it literally wedged itself into Gregor's back. Gregor tried to drag himself on as if this shocking, incredible pain might pass with a change of location, but he felt as though nailed to the spot, and he stretched himself out in complete confusion of all his senses. With his last conscious look, he saw the door of his room being torn open and his mother in her chemise – his sister had partly undressed her to help her breathe more freely in her fainting spell – rushing out ahead of his screaming sister. He saw his mother running up to his father, her loosened petticoats slipping to the floor one by one; and how she, stumbling over her skirts, flung herself upon his father and embraced him in complete union with him – but now Gregor's sight began to fail – imploring him, with her hands clasped around his father's neck, for mercy on Gregor's life.

III

Gregor's serious injury, which caused him more than a month of suffering – the apple remained embedded in his flesh as a visual reminder since no one dared to remove it – seemed to have brought even to his father's attention that Gregor, in spite of his present wretched and revolting shape, was a member of the family, who ought not to be treated as an enemy, but that on the contrary family duty required them to swallow their aversion and to endure, endure, simply endure.

And although Gregor had lost some of his mobility, probably forever because of this injury and for the time being it took him long, long minutes to cross his room like an old invalid – crawling up high was out of the question – for this deterioration of his condition, he was granted what he considered an entirely satisfactory compensation: in that every day toward evening the living room door, which he had made a habit of watching intently for two hours beforehand, was opened, so that lying in the darkness of his room and invisible from the living room, he could see his family at the lamp-lit table and listen to their talk by general consent, as it were, quite differently from how he had done before.

They were, of course, no longer the animated conversations of earlier times, which Gregor had always thought about wistfully in those small hotel rooms when he had had to throw himself wearily into the damp bedding. Now things were mostly very quiet. His father would soon fall asleep in his armchair after supper; his mother and sister would admonish each other to be silent; his mother, leaning far forward under the lamp, sewed fine lingerie for a fashion boutique; his sister, who had taken a job as a salesclerk, was learning shorthand and French in the evenings in order to perhaps obtain a better job later on. Sometimes his father woke up, and as if he had no idea he'd been sleeping, would say to his mother, "What a lot of sewing you're doing again tonight!" and would go right back to sleep again, while mother and sister would smile wearily at each other.

Out of some kind of obstinacy his father refused to take off his messenger's uniform even in the house, and while the dressing gown hung uselessly on the clothes-peg, he slept fully dressed in his chair, as though he were permanently ready for duty and awaiting even here the call of his superior. As a result, his uniform, not new to begin with, began to get dirty despite all the care of Gregor's mother and sister, and Gregor often spent entire evenings gazing at this garment all covered with stains and its constantly polished gold buttons, in which the old man slept most uncomfortably yet peacefully.

As soon as the clock struck ten his mother would try to wake up his father with gentle encouraging words and then persuade him to go to bed, for he was not getting proper sleep here, and he badly needed it since he had to go on duty at six o'clock. But with the obstinacy which had possessed him since he had become a messenger, he always insisted on staying longer at the table although he regularly fell asleep and could then, only after the greatest effort, be persuaded to exchange the armchair for the bed. However much mother and sister might have urged with little admonitions, he would shake his head slowly for a quarter of an hour, keep his eyes closed, and not stand up. Gregor's mother tugged at his sleeve, whispered endearments into his ear; his sister left her homework to help his mother, but his father did not respond. He only sank deeper into his armchair. Not until the women took hold of him under the arms would he open his eyes, look alternately at mother and sister and usually say: "What a life. So this is the peace of my old age." And leaning on the two women he would rise to his feet, laboriously, as if he were his own greatest burden, and let himself be led by the women as far as the door, where he waved them off and proceeded on his own while Gregor's mother abandoned her sewing, and his sister her pen, so as to run after him and be of further help.

Who in this overworked and exhausted family had time to worry about Gregor any more than was absolutely necessary? The household was reduced more and more; the servant girl was now let go after all; a huge, bony charwoman with white hair fluttering about her head came in the mornings and evenings to do the heaviest work; everything else his mother took care of in addition to all her sewing. It even happened that various pieces of family jewelry, which his mother and sister had worn with pleasure at parties and celebrations, were sold, as Gregor discovered one evening from the general discussion of the prices they had obtained. But the greatest complaint was always that they could not give up the flat, which was far too big for their present circumstances, since one could not conceive how Gregor was to be moved. But Gregor understood well enough that it was not only consideration for him which prevented a move, for they could easily have transported him in a suitable crate with a few airholes; what mainly prevented the family from moving was rather their complete hopelessness and the notion that they had been struck by a misfortune such as none of their relatives or acquaintances had ever been. What the world demands of the poor they fulfilled to the utmost, his father brought the minor bank officials their breakfast, his mother sacrificed herself making underwear for strangers, his sister ran back and forth behind the counter at the command of customers, but the strength of the family did not hold out for anything more. And the wound in Gregor's back began to ache anew when mother and sister –

having brought his father to bed – returned, left their work lying, drew close to each other, sat cheek to cheek and his mother, pointing to Gregor's room, said: "Close that door, Grete," and Gregor was once again in darkness while next door the women mingled their tears or perhaps just stared dry-eyed at the table.

Gregor spent the days and nights almost entirely without sleep. Sometimes he thought the next time the door opened he would take the family's affairs into his hands again just as he used to do; once more after a long interval there appeared in his thoughts the boss and the chief clerk, the salesmen and the apprentices, the exceptionally dense errand boy, two or three friends from other firms, a chambermaid from one of the rural hotels – a sweet and fleeting memory; a cashier in a hat shop, whom he had courted earnestly but too slowly – all of them appeared mingled with strangers or people he had already forgotten, but instead of helping him or his family they were all of them inaccessible, and he was glad when they vanished. Then at other times he was not at all in the mood to worry about his family, he was only filled with rage over his poor treatment, and although he couldn't imagine anything he would have felt like eating, he still made plans for getting into the larder to take what was after all his due, even if he wasn't hungry. Without considering anymore what treat Gregor might enjoy, his sister hurriedly pushed any old food into

Gregor's room with her foot before she ran off to work in the morning and afternoon, and in the evening, regardless of whether the food had been only tasted or – as was most often the case – left completely untouched, she swept it out with a sweep of the broom. The cleaning of his room, which she now always did in the evenings, could not have been done more hastily. Streaks of dirt ran along the walls; here and there lay clusters of dust and filth. At first Gregor would place himself upon his sister's arrival in a corner which was particularly indicative of this filth, so as to make his position there a reproach, so to speak. But he could have stayed there for weeks before his sister would have shown any improvement; she saw the dirt as well as he, but she'd simply decided to leave it. At the same time, with a touchiness that was completely new to her, that had in fact affected the whole family, she retained the cleaning of Gregor's room as her preserve. Gregor's mother had on one occasion subjected Gregor's room to a thorough cleaning, which she'd managed only with the use of several buckets of water – all that dampness, of course, irritated Gregor too, and he lay spread out, bitter and motionless, on the sofa – but his mother was not spared any punishment. For hardly had his sister noticed the change in Gregor's room that evening than she ran into the living room deeply insulted, and in spite of her mother's imploringly raised hands, burst into a fit of crying which both parents – his father had, of course, been startled out of his chair – at first watched in helpless amazement until they too got started, his father blaming his mother on the right for not leaving the cleaning of Gregor's room to his sister and screaming at his sister on the left that she would never again be allowed to clean Gregor's room, while his mother tried to drag his father, who was delirious with rage, into the bedroom; his sister, shaken with sobs pounded the table with her small fists; and Gregor hissed loudly with rage because it did not occur to any of them to close the door and spare him such a scene and racket.

But even if his sister, exhausted from her daily job, had grown tired of caring for Gregor as she used to, it would not have been necessary at all for his mother to intervene and for Gregor to become neglected. For the charwoman was now there. This old widow, whose strong bony frame had probably helped her survive the worst in her long life, was not really repelled by Gregor. Without being in any way curious she had once accidentally opened the door to Gregor's room and, at the sight of Gregor – who, completely taken by suprise, began to run back and forth even though no one was chasing him – remained standing in amazement with her hands folded. From then on she never missed a chance to open the door a crack every morning and every evening to have a quick look at Gregor. In the beginning she even used to call him over to her with words she probably considered friendly, such as "Come here a minute, you old dung-beetle!" or "Look at the old dung-beetle!" To such forms of address Gregor made no response but stayed motionless where he was as if the door had not been opened at all. If only this charwoman had been given orders to clean his room daily rather than allowing her to disturb him uselessly according to her mood! Once, early in the morning – heavy rain, perhaps a sign of the approaching spring, was beating against the window panes – Gregor was so exasperated when the charwoman began again with her phrases that he turned on her, as if to attack her, though slowly and feebly to be sure. But the charwoman, instead of being afraid, simply lifted a chair she found near the door high up in the air, and as she stood there with her mouth wide open it was clear that she intended to shut it only when the chair in her hand came crashing down on Gregor's back. "So, you're not coming any closer?" she asked when Gregor turned round again, and she calmly put the chair back in the corner.

Gregor now ate hardly anything anymore. Only when he happened to pass the food laid out for him would he take a bite into his mouth just for fun, hold it there for hours, and then usually spit it out again. At first he thought it was grief over the state of his room which kept him from eating, but it was precisely the changes in his room to which he was soon reconciled. It had become the habit to put things into this room for which no room could be found elsewhere, and there were now plenty of these as one of the rooms of the flat had been rented to three lodgers. These serious gentlemen – all three had full beards as Gregor once observed through a crack in the door – were obsessed with neatness, not only in their room but, since they had now moved in here, in the entire household and in particular in the kitchen. They could not tolerate useless let alone dirty junk. Moreover, they had brought along most of their own household goods. For this reason many things had become superfluous, which though they were admittedly not saleable could hardly be thrown away either. All of these things wandered into Gregor's room; likewise, the ash bucket and the garbage bin from the kitchen. Anything that was not being used for the moment was simply flung into Gregor's room by the charwoman, who was always in a great hurry; luckily, Gregor usually saw only the object in question and the hand that held it. It was possible the charwoman had intended to reclaim things in time and on occasion or else throw everything away at one go, but in fact they just remained where they had first landed except when Gregor wound his way through the junk and set it in motion, at first out of necessity because there was no other space left for crawling but later with growing amusement, although after such excursions, dead-tired and sad, he didn't move again for hours.

Since the lodgers sometimes also had their dinner at home in the common living room, the living room door stayed shut on certain evenings; but Gregor very easily did without the opening of the door; for on several evenings when it had been opened he had not taken advantage of it but had lain, without the family's noticing, in the darkest corner of his room. But on one occasion the charwoman had left the door to the living room slightly ajar, and it stayed so even when the lodgers came in in the evening and the lamp was lit. They sat down at the top end of the table where in the old days father, mother and Gregor had sat, unfolded their napkins and picked up their knives and forks. At once his mother appeared in the doorway with a dish of meat, and right behind her was his sister, with a bowl piled high with potatoes. The food was steaming with thick vapour. The lodgers bent over the dishes set before them, as if to examine them before eating, and in fact the one sitting in the middle, whom the other two seemed to regard as the authority, cut into a piece of the meat still on the dish, evidently to determine if it was tender enough or whether it shouldn't perhaps be sent back into the kitchen. He was satisfied, and mother and sister, who had been watching anxiously, sighed with relief and began to smile.

The family itself ate in the kitchen. Nonetheless, before going into the kitchen, his father came into the living-room and with a single bow, cap in hand, made a round of the table. The lodgers all rose as one and mumbled something into their beards. When they were alone again, they ate in almost complete silence. It seemed strange to Gregor that of all the various eating noises, he could always pick out the sound of their chewing teeth, as if to demonstrate to Gregor that one needed teeth to eat and that even with the finest toothless jaws, you could do nothing. "I'm hungry," said Gregor sadly to himself, "but not for these things. Look how these lodgers are feeding themselves, and I'm dying."

On this same evening – Gregor could not recall ever having heard the violin the whole time – the sound of violin playing came from the kitchen. The lodgers had already finished their evening meal; the one in the middle had produced a newspaper, given a page each to the other two, and now, leaning back, they read and smoked. When the violin began to play they became attentive, got to their feet, and went on tiptoe to the hall door, where they stood in a huddle. They must have been heard from the kitchen for Gregor's father called out: "Is the playing disturbing you at all, gentlemen? It can be stopped at once." "On the contrary," said the middle lodger, "wouldn't the young lady like to come in to us and play here, where it is much cozier and more comfortable?" "Oh, certainly," called Gregor's father, as if he were the violin player. The lodgers stepped back into the room and waited.

Soon his father came in with the music stand, his mother with the notes and his sister with the violin. His sister quietly got everything ready for playing; his parents, who had never rented out rooms before and who therefore treated the lodgers with excessive politeness, did not even dare to sit down in their own chairs; his father leaned against the door, his right hand inserted between two buttons of his buttoned up livery coat; his mother, however, was offered an armchair by one of the gentlemen and since she left the chair where he had happened to put it, sat in a corner off to one side.

His sister began to play; father and mother from either side attentively followed the movements of her hands. Gregor, attracted by the playing, had ventured forward a little and already had his head in the living room. It hardly surprised him that he was showing so little consideration for the others lately; previously such consideration had been his pride. And yet he had more reason now than ever to keep himself hidden, for because of all the dust which lay all over his room and flew about at the slightest movement, he too was completely covered in dust; fluff, hair, and remnants of food trailed from his back and sides; his indifference to everything was far too great for him to have lain on his back and scrubbed himself clean on the carpet as once he had done several times a day. And in spite of his condition he had no shame in advancing a little on the spotless floor of the living room.

To be sure, nobody paid any attention to him. The family was completely absorbed by the violin playing; the lodgers, on the contrary, who had at first stationed themselves, hands in pockets, much too close behind his sister's music stand, so that they could all have read the music, which surely must have bothered his sister, soon withdrew to the window, chatting to each other in low tones with bent down heads where they stayed anxiously watched by his father. It now seemed only too obvious that they had been disappointed in their expectation of hearing beautiful or entertaining violin playing, had had enough of the whole performance and only continued to let their peace be disturbed out of politeness. Especially the manner in which they all blew the cigar smoke through nose and mouth high in the air suggested great nervousness. And yet his sister was playing so beautifully. Her face was tilted to one side; with a searching and sad look in her eyes she followed the notes of music. Gregor crawled a little farther forward, holding his head close to the floor so that it might be possible for their eyes to meet. Was he an animal that music could move him so? He felt as if the way to the unknown nourishment he craved was opening before him. He was determined to push on until he reached his sister, tug at her skirt and so indicate to her that she should come into his room with her violin, for here no one was worthy of her playing as he would be worthy of it. He would never again let her out of his room, at least not for as long as he lived; his terrifying shape would be of use to him for the first time; he would be at all the doors of his room at the same time hissing and spitting at all intruders; his sister, however, should not be forced to stay with him but do so freely; she should sit beside him on the sofa, bend down her ear to him and then he would confide to her that he had had the firm intention of sending her to the Conservatory, and that, if this catastrophe had not intervened, he would have announced this to everyone last Christmas – surely Christmas was already past? – without concerning himself with any objections. After this declaration his sister would be so moved that she would burst into tears, and Gregor would raise himself up to her shoulder and kiss her neck, which ever since she started going to work she kept free of any ribbon or collar.

"Mr. Samsa!" cried the middle lodger to Gregor's father, and without wasting another word, pointed with his index finger at the slowly approaching Gregor. The violin fell silent; the middle lodger first smiled to his friends shaking his head and then looked again at Gregor. His father seemed to think it more urgent to first calm down the lodgers rather than to drive Gregor out, although they were not at all upset, and Gregor seemed to be entertaining them more than all the violinplaying. He hurried toward them, and with arms outstretched tried to drive them back into their room and to block their view of Gregor with his body. Now they really did become a little angry; it was not clear whether because of his father's behaviour or because of the realization which now dawned on them, that they had unwittingly had such a next door neighbour as Gregor. They demanded explanations from his father, raised their arms in turn, tugged uneasily at their beards and reluctantly retreated toward their room. His sister had in the meantime emerged from the state of abstraction into which she had lapsed after her playing had been so suddenly interrupted; after holding the violin and bow for a while in her slackly hanging hands, and continuing to look at the music as if she were still playing, she had suddenly pulled herself together, laid the instrument into the lap of her mother – who was still sitting in her chair fighting for breath, her lungs heaving violently – and had run into the adjoining room, which the lodgers were nearing all the more quickly under the urging of his father. One could see the blankets and cushions on the beds fly in the air under the practiced hands of his sister and arrange themselves in order. Before the lodgers had even reached the room, she had finished making the beds and slipped out. His father seemed once again so possessed by his obstinacy that he forgot all the respect he nevertheless owed his tenants. He just kept pushing and shoving until, already at the door of the bedroom, the middle lodger stamped his food thunderously, thereby bringing him to a standstill.

"I hereby declare," he said, raising his hand and casting his eyes around for mother and sister too, "that in view of the disgusting conditions prevailing in this flat and family" – here he spat decisively on the floor – "I am giving immediate notice. Naturally, I will not pay the slightest even for the days I've lived here; on the contrary, I will consider taking some kind of action against you with claims that, believe me, will be very easy to substantiate." He stopped and stared straight ahead of him as if expecting something. And indeed his two friends at once chimed in with the words: "We too, are giving immediate notice." With that he grabbed the door handle and shut the door with a bang.

Gregor's father staggered with groping hands to his armchair and collapsed into it; it looked as if he were stretching himself out for his usual evening nap, but the intense nodding of his head, as if it had lost all support, showed that he was far from sleeping. All this time Gregor had been lying quietly on the spot where the lodgers had caught sight of him. His disappointment at the failure of his plan, but perhaps also the weakness caused him by extreme hunger, made it impossible for him to move. He feared with a degree of certainty that in the very next moment a general collapse would overcome him, and he waited. Not even the violin startled him when it slipped from under the trembling fingers of his mother and fell from her lap with a resounding tone.

"Dear parents," said his sister, slamming her hand on the table by way of introduction, "things can't go on like this. Perhaps you don't realize that, but I do. I will not utter the name of my brother in front of this monster, and so all I say is: we have to try to get rid of it. We've done everything humanly possible to take care of it and to put up with it; I don't think anyone can reproach us in the slightest."

"She's right a thousand times over," said his father to himself. His mother, who could still not catch her breath, began to cough a hollow cough into her hand with a wild look in her eyes.

His sister rushed over to his mother and held her forehead. His father's thoughts seemed to have become clearer at the words of his sister; he had sat himself upright and was playing with his uniform cap among the plates which were still lying on the table from the lodgers' supper, and from time to time he looked at the motionless form of Gregor.

"We must try to get rid of it," said his sister, now exclusively to his father since her mother couldn't hear anything for her coughing, "it'll be the death of you both; I can see it coming. When one has to work as hard as we all do, then one can't endure this constant torment at home too. At least I can't stand it anymore." And she broke into such bitter sobbing that her tears fell down onto her mother's face, where she wiped them away with mechanical hand movements.

"Child," said her father sympathetically, and with noticeable understanding, "but what are we to do?"

Gregor's sister only shrugged her shoulders as a sign of the helplessness which had taken hold of her during her fit of weeping in contrast to her earlier confidence.

"If he could understand us," said her father half-questioningly; Gregor's sister, still sobbing, waved her hand vehemently as a sign that this was out of the question.

"If he could understand us," repeated her father and by closing his eyes absorbed his daughter's conviction of the impossibility of this, "then perhaps we might be able to come to an agreement with him. But as things are..."

"He has to go," cried his sister, "that's the only solution, father. You just have to try to get rid of the idea that it's Gregor. That we believed it for so long, that is our real tragedy. But how can it be Gregor? If it were Gregor, he would have realized long since that it isn't possible for human beings to live together with such a creature, and he would have gone away of his own accord. Then we wouldn't have a brother, but we would be able to go on living and honour his memory. But as it is, this animal persecutes us, drives away the lodgers and obviously wants to occupy the whole flat and have us sleep in the gutter. Just look, father," she suddenly shrieked. "He's at it again!" And in a fit of terror completely incomprehensible to Gregor she even abandoned her mother, literally thrust herself from her chair as if she would rather sacrifice her mother than stay near Gregor, and rushed behind her father, who, upset only by her behaviour, also stood up and half raised his arms in front of her as though to protect her.

But Gregor had not the slightest intention of frightening anyone, least of all his sister. He had only started to turn himself around so he could wander back into his room, and this certainly did look peculiar since because of his disabled condition he had to use his head, which he lifted several times and knocked against the floor to help with the difficult turning manoeuvre. He paused and looked around. His good intentions appeared to have been recognized; it had only been a momentary scare. Now they all looked silently and sadly at him. His mother lay in her armchair with her legs outstretched and pressed together, her eyes almost closing from exhaustion; his father and sister sat beside each other, and his sister had put her arm around her father's neck.

"Perhaps now I'm allowed to turn around," thought Gregor and set to work again. He couldn't suppress the panting from the effort, and had to rest now and then. Otherwise no one harrassed him; it was all left entirely to him. When he had completed the turn he began at once to wander back in a straight line. He was amazed at the great distance separating him from his room and could not understand at all how in his weak state he had covered the same distance a short time ago almost without noticing it. All the while intent on just crawling quickly, he hardly noticed that not a word, not an exclamation from his family was disturbing him. Only when he was already in the doorway did he turn his head; not completely, for he felt his neck stiffening; nevertheless, he still saw that nothing had changed behind him except that his sister had stood up. His last glance was of his mother, who was by now fast asleep.

He was hardly inside his room when the door was promptly slammed shut, bolted and locked. The sudden noise behind him startled Gregor so much that his little legs gave way beneath him. It was his sister who had been in such a hurry. She had been standing there ready and waiting; then she had sprung forward nimbly. Gregor had not even heard her coming, and she cried out, "Finally!" to her parents as she turned the key in the lock.

"And now?" Gregor asked himself, looking round him in the darkness. He soon made the discovery that he was now unable to move at all. This did not surprise him; rather it struck him as unnatural that he had until now been able to move on these thin little legs at all. Otherwise, he felt relatively comfortable. True, he had pains all over his body, but it seemed to him that they were gradually growing less and less and would finally pass away altogether.

The rotting apple in his back and the inflamed area around it, completely covered with soft dust, hardly bothered him anymore. He thought back to his family with tenderness and love. His own opinion that he would have to disappear was, if possible, even firmer than his sister's. He remained in this state of vacant and peaceful reflection until the tower clock struck three in the morning. He still experienced the first signs of the general brightening outside his window. Then his head sank all the way down without his consent, and his last breath flowed faintly out of his nostrils.

When the charwoman arrived early in the morning – out of sheer energy and impatience she slammed all the doors so hard, however often one had asked her not to, that no peaceful sleep in the entire flat was possible after her arrival – she didn't notice anything out of the ordinary during her usual short visit to Gregor. She thought he was lying there motionless on purpose, pretending that his feelings were hurt; she credited him with all kinds of cunning. Since she happened to have the long broom in her hand, she tried to tickle Gregor with it from the door. When that too produced no results, she became annoyed and jabbed into Gregor a little, and only when she had pushed him from his place without meeting any resistance, did she begin to take notice. When she soon grasped the true state of things, her eyes widened, and she let out a whistle but did not delay rather, she tore open the door to the bedroom and yelled at the top of her voice into the darkness: "Come and have a look; it's dropped dead; it's lying there, dead and done for."

The couple, Mr. and Mrs. Samsa, sat up in bed and had enough to do to get over the shock of the charwoman before finally managing to grasp her message. But then Mr. and Mrs. Samsa hurriedly climbed out of bed, each on their own side; Mr. Samsa threw the blanket over his shoulders, and Mrs. Samsa came out in nothing but her nightgown; dressed thus they stepped into Gregor's room. In the meantime the door of the living room, where Grete had been sleeping since the lodgers had moved in, had also opened; she was completely dressed as if she had not slept at all, and her pale face seemed to confirm it. "Dead?" said Mrs. Samsa, and looked inquiringly at the charwoman although she could have checked everything for herself and could even recognize the truth without doing so. "I should say so," said the charwoman, and to prove it she pushed Gregor's corpse a good stretch to the side with her broom. Mrs. Samsa made a movement as if to hold back the broom, but didn't. "Well," said Mr. Samsa, "now thanks be to God." He crossed himself, and the three women followed his example. Grete, whose eyes never left the corpse, said: "Just look how thin he was. He didn't eat anything for such a long time. The food came out again just as it had gone in." Indeed, Gregor's body was completely flat and dry; this could be seen for the first time now since it was no longer raised up on its little legs, and nothing else distracted the eye.

"Come in with us a little while, Grete," said Mrs. Samsa with a sad smile, and Grete, not without looking back at the corpse, followed her parents into the bedroom. The charwoman closed the door and opened the window wide. Although it was early in the morning, there was already a certain mildness mixed with the fresh air. After all, it was already the end of March.

The three lodgers stepped out of their room and looked around in surprise for their breakfast; they had been forgotten. "Where is breakfast?" the middle gentleman sullenly asked the charwoman. But she put her finger to her lips and then hastily and silently beckoned the men to come into Gregor's room. They did so and then stood, their hands in the pockets of their somewhat shabby coats, around Gregor's body in the now already fully-lit room.

At that point the door of the bedroom opened and Mr. Samsa appeared in his uniform, his wife on one arm, his daughter on the other. They all looked as though they had been crying a little; now and then Grete pressed her face against her father's sleeve.

"Leave my house at once!" said Mr. Samsa and pointed to the door without letting go of the women. "How do you mean that?" said the middle lodger somewhat taken aback, and smiled a sugary smile. The two others held their hands behind their backs and incessantly rubbed them together as if in gleeful anticipation of a major confrontation which would only turn out in their favour. "I mean exactly what I say," answered Mr. Samsa, and with his two escorts advanced in a straight line toward the lodger. At first the lodger stood still looking at the floor as if his thoughts were rearranging themselves in a new order. "Well then, I guess we'll go," he said, and looked up at Mr. Samsa as though in a sudden fit of humility he required fresh permission even for this decision. Mr. Samsa merely nodded briefly, glaring at him several times. Thereupon the gentleman really did go into the hall immediately, taking long strides. His two friends had been listening closely for a while already, their hands still, and now went hopping right after him as though afraid that Mr. Samsa could step into the hall before them and cut them off from their leader. In the front hall all three took their hats from the coat rack in the front room, pulled their sticks from the umbrella stand, bowed in silence and left the flat. In what turned out to be a completely unfounded suspicion, Mr. Samsa followed with the two women out onto the landing; leaning against the banister, they watched the three gentlemen slowly but surely descending the long flight of stairs, disappearing on each floor at a particular turn of the stairway and after a few moments reappearing;

the lower they got the more the Samsas lost interest in them, and when a butcher's boy with a tray on his head came climbing up the stairs past them with a proud bearing, Mr. Samsa and the women soon let go of the banister, and all turned back as if relieved, into their flat.

They decided to spend this day resting and going for a stroll; they had not only earned such a respite from work, they absolutely needed it. And so they sat down at the table and wrote three letters of apology, Mr. Samsa to the management of his bank, Mrs. Samsa to her employer and Grete to the store owner. While they were writing the charwoman came in to say that she was leaving since her morning's work was finished. The three letter writers simply nodded at first without looking up, but as the charwoman kept lingering there, they looked up, annoyed. "Well?" asked Mr. Samsa. The charwoman stood smiling in the doorway as though she had some great good news to tell the family but would only do so if she were thoroughly questioned. The little ostrich feather, which stood almost upright on her hat and had irritated Mr. Samsa the whole time she'd been with them, swayed gently in all directions. "Well, what is it you want, then?" asked Mrs. Samsa, for whom the charwoman had the most respect. "Well," the charwoman answered and for good-natured laughing could not immediately continue, "just to tell you that you don't have to worry about how to get rid of that thing next door. It's already been taken care of." Mrs. Samsa and Grete bent down over their letters as if to continue writing; Mr. Samsa, who perceived that the charwoman was about to start describing everything in detail, stopped her decisively with an outstretched arm. As she wasn't allowed to tell her story, she remembered the great hurry she was in and called out obviously offended, "Bye, everyone," whirled around violently and left the flat with a terrible slamming of doors.

"She'll be let go tonight," said Mr. Samsa, but received no answer from either his wife or his daughter for the charwoman seemed to have shattered their barely regained peace of mind. They got up, went to the window and stayed there clasping each other tight. Mr. Samsa turned around in his chair towards them and watched them quietly for a while. Then he called out: "Come on now, come here. Stop brooding over the past once and for all. And have a little consideration for me too." The women complied at once, hurried over to him, cuddled him and quickly finished their letters.

Then all three of them together left the flat, something they had not done in months, and took the tram into the open country on the outskirts of the city. The tramcar, in which they were the only passengers, was completely filled with warm sunshine. Leaning comfortably back in their seats they discussed their prospects for the future, and it appeared on closer inspection that these were by no means bad, for all three jobs, which they had never really asked each other about in detail, were extremely favourable and especially promising for the future. The greatest immediate improvement in their situation would, of course, come about easily through a change of residence; they would now take a smaller and cheaper but a better located and altogether more manageable flat than the current one, which Gregor had chosen. While they were thus conversing, it occurred to Mr. and Mrs. Samsa almost at the same moment at the sight of their increasingly lively daughter, that despite all the troubles which had turned her cheeks pale, she had recently blossomed into a pretty and shapely girl. Growing quieter and communicating almost unconsciously by an exchange of glances, they thought that it would soon be time to find her a good husband. And it was like a confirmation of their new dreams and good intentions when at the end of the journey their daughter was the first to rise to her feet and stretch her young body.

Karl Brand*

The Retransformation of Gregor Samsa

That dreadful bug corpse of Gregor Samsa had been removed by a knacker's cart. This had, with the help of assistants, driven the dry and emaciated body out of the city and dumped it onto a monstrous rubbish heap. It is not known how long the dead, decomposing body had been waiting there alone for the burial, however, under the influence of the sun's heat it had already begun to emit a foul, horrible smell. The great swarm of flies which teemed around the monstrous rubbish heap during the day didn't dare approach this terrible form nor its stench.

The sun inched its way down behind the hills surrounding the city, and a cool dew began to descend at nightfall so that the bug body of the dead Gregor Samsa was completely covered with large drops of dew.

But for the impervious darkness, the paper and old broken stone and metal pots lying around him might have noticed that Gregor Samsa's three exposed little legs suddenly began to quiver, yet they wouldn't have attached any importance to this quivering since they would have assumed that it was the wind which was stirring his limbs. This was, however, not the case. On the contrary: a strange something began to flow through Gregor Samsa's corpse, from which emerged a sudden ability to think that expressed itself immediately and perpetually in the single sentence: "Tomorrow, I will pull myself together and present myself to them." This line of thought did not proceed any further, nor could Gregor Samsa even decipher what this strange sentence was supposed to mean.

Hours passed. After their passage, however, he was able to become master enough of his thoughts that after a terrible effort he at least acquired the will to get away from there. As his thoughts began in the course of time to collect themselves more and more and to arrange themselves together into a single long chain, he noted to his horror that a great, incredible transformation was taking place in his bug body. He couldn't identify it, but rather had only the feeling that his back pair of limbs, and with them his entire body, had begun to get longer in an inexplicable manner.

And thus the terrible awareness came to Gregor Samsa that he was alive, had until recently been considered dead and had for years been transformed into an enormous, hideous bug. It had been so long since he had had these thoughts. He tried to ascertain about how many days might have elapsed since his supposed death and his present awakening.

Then he told himself that he must stay calm until daybreak again and then decide by daylight what else should be done. But he was still trying to ascertain where he could now possibly be and noticed that he was lying in something soft. He still didn't dare use his limbs. It couldn't be a bed he was lying in, straw or hay much less so. But his breathing became slower, and since he was lying almost completely face down he found himself compelled first to raise his head, and since he couldn't continue to hold it up stiff, turned his torso all the way to the side. At this he discovered to his astonishment that two of his limbs fell off painlessly. He propped himself up. In doing so it seemed to him that he had hands. A tortuous desire to stand erect on his two lower limbs overwhelmed him, but he was in the end too cowardly to imagine that he could have assumed a human shape again.

Time was slowly creeping past him. He listened expectantly to see if he would hear one of the suburban church clocks strike. He lay motionless on his side and listened. Then it struck a quarter of the hour. After a long, tedious, wait, he heard the clock strike half, then three-quarters of the hour before it finally struck three. A shiver passed through him.

He thought: "Well, another one and a half hours before it is day and with it the light." He didn't want to think. But again and again the long, agonizing cycle of his thoughts kept returning. The mere idea that something had happened to *him and that he – and he trembled in fear throughout his whole gaunt body – had reassumed human form was becoming clearer to Gregor with every minute. He finally bent his upper limbs to his forehead and beat his temples in despair. He felt with horror that he had fingers, human hands.*

He gathered all his dormant strength and sprang to his feet. The darkness was still thick and impenetrable and he could not even see a path the width of a hand in front of him. "Walk," it occurred to him. And he tried to walk. But his knees shook. He could hardly keep his balance; and whenever he wanted to put his foot forward a step, he fell to the ground again. His face became hot, an icy cold passed over his back, and he felt feverish. How was he to get home? Pain and weakness forced him to remain lying motionless. An unspeakable fear that he would die overwhelmed him.

His churning inner being resisted this thought.

He remembered his misery: "Has anyone suffered as much as I have? No one. Now I'm old and have no life behind me that I could call a life."

He felt a burning pain in his back. His fingers touched the spot. Only now did Gregor Samsa recall that it was the wound which his father had inflicted upon him, when, in a rage he threw an apple at him.

With the morning's first ray of light, which fell upon him and enabled him to see his human form, he began to give the following speech:

"Herald of the day! The great sorrow which I've lived through has made me a human being once again. I've never before thought about destiny, but now I'm learning to contemplate it. Destiny would have me go up to these people whom I call father, mother, sister, boss and colleagues and who had no need of me because my body was rotting, who hated and feared me, who out of shame in front of the others hid me and whose hatred went so far that they pounded wounds into my body.

"Father! How shall I now stand before you without avenging my pain and suffering upon you? Without cursing you? My life was no life. It was an immeasurable misery which did

not know youth or joy. Now I'm a human being once again. Almost an old man, weak and unsteady. And I don't know anything except that my entire being is in a state of great wretchedness – a single unfathomable, eternally all-encompassing yearning. I don't know anything but that I am now weak and freezing."

And he lay silent on the ground, pondering and waiting to see if his weakness, which still held him in chains, would disappear. The great silence which surrounded him now spread about a great peace, and his heart was calm and full of goodness.

The sun crept slowly up its heavenly path and spread a gentle warmth around him. Gregor Samsa lay silent and still against the ethereal arch of the sky which wordlessly and silently, and heard only by him, spoke to him: "Stand up! Go now."

And Gregor Samsa rose to his feet and went. His steps were slow but firm and unrelenting. And when he arrived at the first buildings of the city, the rows of houses cried out to him:

"A new life is beginning!"

---

*) Brand, Karl – *15.10.1895 in Witkowitz (Moravia), †17.3.1917 in Prague. An expressionist, today an almost forgotten poet from the circle of Franz Kafka. The story, "The Retransformation of Gregor Samsa" which was published in the "Prager Tagblatt" 11 June 1916, depicts the identification of the young Karl Brand, ill with tuberculosis, with the central figure of Franz Kafka's "Metamorphosis" and became a much discussed testimony of the strong effect of the story on contemporary readers. The destiny of the poet Brand, whose artistic achievements were discovered by Johannes Urzidil and Franz Werfel especially, shows surprising parallels to those of Gregor Samsa: "Everyone is working because of me, for I am the parasite who is consuming money which one could set aside or spend sensibly. I'm lying there or crawling around, bug- or dung-beetle-like and good for nothing."